The Most Famous Fables

From Aesop, Phaedras, La Fontaine, and Krylov

By Alex Wolf Neuk

Illustrated by Mariana Hnatenko

Produced by Alina Shabelnyk

Publisher:
Fabulous Book Company / Fabulous Trust
P.O. Box 572, Bondi Junction NSW 1355, Australia
enquiries@mostfamousfables.com

ABN: 37 501 997 237

This book belongs to

....

....

Table of Contents

To My Reader

Fables are fabulous by definition
Containing millennia's worth of tradition
Out of history, myths, superstition
On human nature and human condition.
Start reading - it's a wild ride!
With wild animals inside.

I meet them often when I write
So rest assured, they will not bite.
There every lion, crow, and fox,
Frog, rabbit, antelope, and ox,
Ass, goat, kangaroo, and possum,
Though not a human, is a person
With character and with intent,
Delight, indifference, contempt,
Endowed with feelings, thoughts, and souls,
Ambitions, aspirations, goals.
Without offense can take a joke
Like a bug in a rug
or a pig in a poke.

Read, listen, try to understand,
Discern satire, humour, and
Sometimes to memory commit;
Sharpen your reason and your wit.

Fables are fabulous by definition -
See for yourself when you read this edition!
They can be spicy and effervescent,
They can be great antidepressants.
They can be memorized with ease,
They go well with wine and cheese.
They can be used for noble ends:
Surprise and entertain your friends!

And if I'm not underperforming
All those fabulists before me,
Give me credit, shout Encore!
I shall be glad to publish more.

The Fox and the Crow

The Crow procured a piece of cheese,
Sat on a perch among the trees
And contemplated what a treat
This piece of cheese would be to eat.

The Fox in passing and with ease,
Smelled the aroma in the breeze.
He stopped, looked up, and saw the Crow
And very sweetly said:
"Hello!
Oh! What a beauty to behold!
Such grace and qualities untold!
A veritable beauty queen
These parts have never, ever seen.

So dark, so handsome, and streamlined,
So graceful, cultured, and refined,
With so beautiful a shine,
So indisputably divine.

Yet such a modest pretty thing.
If I could only hear you sing…
Anticipating your fine trill
I can already feel a thrill."

The Crow, not known to be coy,
Was now beside herself with joy.
She croaked a loud cawing shriek
And let the cheese fall from her beak.

The Fox watching the cheese fall,
Made off with it in no time at all.

It is expedient to scoff
At crows easily cheesed off.

The moral here is what seems to matter:
Sometimes it really pays to flatter.

Sour Grapes

The Fox in terrible affront
Came empty-handed from the hunt.
He'd hurt his body and his pride,
His hungry stomach hurt inside.

By grace apparently divine,
He stumbled on a rich grapevine.
Bright, crystal garnets sprayed with dew,
Inviting, sparkling in full view!

A whet for any appetite,
The only drawback was their height.

The Fox, filled with determination,
Could not resist such a temptation.
He jumped up high and tried to pinch,
But missed them by about an inch.

He jumped again, and then again;
There was no gain but only pain.

He worked himself into a sweat
For what he saw, but could not get,
For what he smelled, but couldn't taste,
And all his efforts went to waste.
The luckless Fox after an hour
Decided: "Those grapes are sour.
Too green, too tart, a bad suggestion,
I wouldn't want the indigestion."

The Old Lion

A sorry picture is before us:
The Lion, terror of the forest,
Under the burden of his age
Has lost his prowess and his rage.

His subjects - jealous of his wealth -
Emboldened by his loss of health
Attack him openly.

The Horse
Has kicked him twice without remorse.

As vengeance or out of spite,
The Wolf is very keen to bite.
Perhaps to settle an old score,
The Oxen take their chance to gore.
The Lion, while expecting more,
With dignity, without fear,
Knows very well his end is near.

He sits resigned, without complaint,
Quietly praying to his Saint,
Awaiting destiny.
But then
He sees the Ass approach his den.

The Ass won't pass his claim to fame.
Just like the others takes his aim
And is about to strike a blow,
But then the Lion roars in woe:

"It does not have to get this low!
I pray that I may quickly go.
Death might be cruel but alas,
It's better than an insult from an ass."

The Lion's Share

Good will and common sense applying,
The Dog, the Fox, the Wolf, the Lion
Agreed to bury the tradition
Of fierce, cut-throat competition.

They realized it would be great
If they could all cooperate.
They'd maximize their forces
By pooling their resources
And then - to even out the score -
They'd split the prey between the four.

As is the custom among free men,
They put a seal to their agreement.

The Dog was first to trap a bear
And called his partners in to share.

The Lion, as the most able,
Had pride of place at their table.
He said: "Before the banquet starts,
We'll split the prey into four parts.

The contract we agreed to sign,
States clearly: the first part's mine.
I am the hungriest, I reckon,
So I should also have the second.
And I recall an old decree:
He who has two can then have three.
I'll also have the fourth because
Around here I make the laws.
I am the king, lest you forget it,
And he who argues will regret it."

By Lion's rule it's only fair
The Lion gets the Lion's share.

The Wolf and the Crane

The Wolf has always been a glutton.
Once, after feasting on some mutton,
Followed by venison, and goat,
A bone got stuck deep in his throat.

The Wolf, so desperate in strife,
In mortal fear for his life
Cried out for help and gave his word
To pay a generous reward.

The Crane by chance was nearby,
And heard the Wolf's exhausted cry,
Took to his heart the Wolf's appeal,
He liked to help and liked the deal.

He then, without hesitation
Proceeded with the operation:
Looked down the throat,
Stuck his long beak in it
And fished the bone out in a minute.

Thus having finished the Crane asked:
"My Lord,
Now about my reward?"

"Your what?
Please do not make me laugh!
As if it wasn't quite enough
To have your neck out of my gullet
In one piece!
What callousness, what greed,
What avarice.

Such disrespect!
Is it because
You managed to escape my claws?

Take my advice, ungrateful Crane:
Don't fall into my paws again."

The Wolf and the Lamb

Does might trump right?
Does reason help you in a fight
Against an overwhelming might?

From pure, sparkling mountain stream
The young Lamb was quenching thirst.
The stream was clear, fresh, and clean,
The Young Lamb was there first.

The Wolf so hungry on the prowl,
He saw the Lamb
As fair game,
And that the Lamb
Should also bear the blame.
And nothing less will do than crying foul:
"How dare you to so much as think
To with impunity pollute my drink ?
Such boldness, such temerity, such nerve
The strictest punishment deserve!"

"Do not be angry Sir,
I certainly expect
Your point of view be treated with respect.

Perhaps your anger, Sir, is just a touch extreme,
Just take a look -I am twenty paces downstream.

Unjustifiably, your anger is inflamed
I can't be blamed..."

"Of course, You should be blamed
For this and spreading lies about me last year"
"Last year? But I wasn't even here,
I am too young, still suckling on my mother"-
"And, if not you,
It must have been your brother!"

"I don't have siblings..."-

"Someone from your tribe;
They wouldn't spare me, no matter what I tried.
Yourself, your shepherds, or your hounds
Can't be as innocent as it so often sounds,
Someone has sinned amongst you all and sundry!
You are to blame, not least, because I'm hungry!
Some things you just cannot undo."

That being said, and not much else to do
The Wolf, without much ado,
Pounced on the Lamb and ate
It up sans sympathy or hate.
Just as due process would mandate.

Not being strong is quite a plight
Try being harmless, innocent, polite.
Within good reason or indeed despite,
It still turns out might is always right!

The Scapegoat

Without premonition, sign, or omen,
Nobody really saw it coming.
Imported from beyond the seas
By "powers that be" displeased
or punishment from God Almighty
For utter lawlessness and fighting.

A plague descended on the realm of beasts
Not least because of their unending feasts.
Their gross intemperance, excesses of consumption,
Without remorse, repentance, or compunction.

Some dead already, others moribund
About to meet their sorry, gory end.
They cough their lungs out, drowning in phlegm
Wondering why this plague came down on them,
What have they done to be in such a way condemned?

The Lion gave counsel when he said:
"My friends,
I think it all depends
on what the Heaven sends
As punishment to us for our sins,
Which may explain the troubles we are in.

For some of us have sinned a lot.
Some more than others, but I know not
Exactly how, who, and what
Each one is guilty of—or not.
I say this body should assess
Degree of guilt once all confess.
Let each atone for his deeds, in turn
Admit, disclose, and affirm
By being penitent and honest,
Confess who brought this deadly plague upon us!

And list of course in your confessions
Misdeeds, trespasses, and transgressions.
Express remorse, contrition, and regret,
And you can hope, pray, or bet
That Gods above who mean and see well
Rule to deliver us from evil.

Plead to be favourably viewed!
Self-sacrifice for common good!

As for myself, I will be blunt
I am a predator, I hunt.
I've taken sheep, hyena, leopard,
And once I even took a shepherd."

Transfixed with tension and suspense
The Fox appeared for the defense:
"Of course,
There's no use denying
That there's been a bit of dying.
Consistent!
With the trade you're plying,
And your position as a lion.
As such your deeds do not exceed
Your range, authority, and need,
And no greater is your guilt
Than that of those you have killed.
We know you well and in a sense
You just confirmed your innocence!"

The Wolf, the Jackal, and the Bear
Among the others were also there.
Through luck , good reason, or collusion
They all got off with similar conclusions.

The Fox's reason, charm, and flair
Acclaimed as just, exemplary, and fair.

At last it was the Goat's turn,
He said: "I fear for this I'll burn
In hell in the infernal flame,
I probably deserve the blame.
You know that meadow by the brook,
I plucked some grass when no one looked."

The Fox, being a good sport,
Appeared now as a friend of the court:
"We could forgive this, but alas,
The Goat devoured the grass.
Protected grass from someone else's lawn;
So lush and harmless, so untimely, gone!

Even attempting a defense
Makes absolutely no sense,
This is a capital offence!
For every argument is flawed
When grass is simply outlawed.

The law about this is straight,
A wasteful shame to litigate.
No need to argue or debate.
To think that those who perpetrate
As grave a felony as ruining landscape
Will proper punishment escape?

From the confessions we heard here,
The Goat's transgressions are severe.
The Goat should not seem or appear
To escape the justice of his peers."

The verdict read, the execution neared.
The verdict's guilty as we feared.
Just after sentencing the goat disappeared,
Devoured by the crowd in the nick of time.
The punishment must always fit the crime!

The Rabbit and the Snail

The Snail wasn't in the habit
Of racing, till one day the Rabbit
For money was on tenterhooks,

Invited punters to make book.
The Rabbit didn't want much risk,
So wouldn't race anyone brisk.
He thought a race against the Snail
Would be impossible to fail.
He also had to test his mettle,
And had a private bet to settle.
A safe, assured bet for the Rabbit
And such an easy way to grab it.

The Snail was slow but never late,
She didn't have much on her plate.
With reputation not at stake
And no records set to break
The Snail wasn't out to win,
But on a dare, would be in.

With that in mind they called a race
And settled on the time and place:
From here to the nearest tree,
And gave it until half past three.

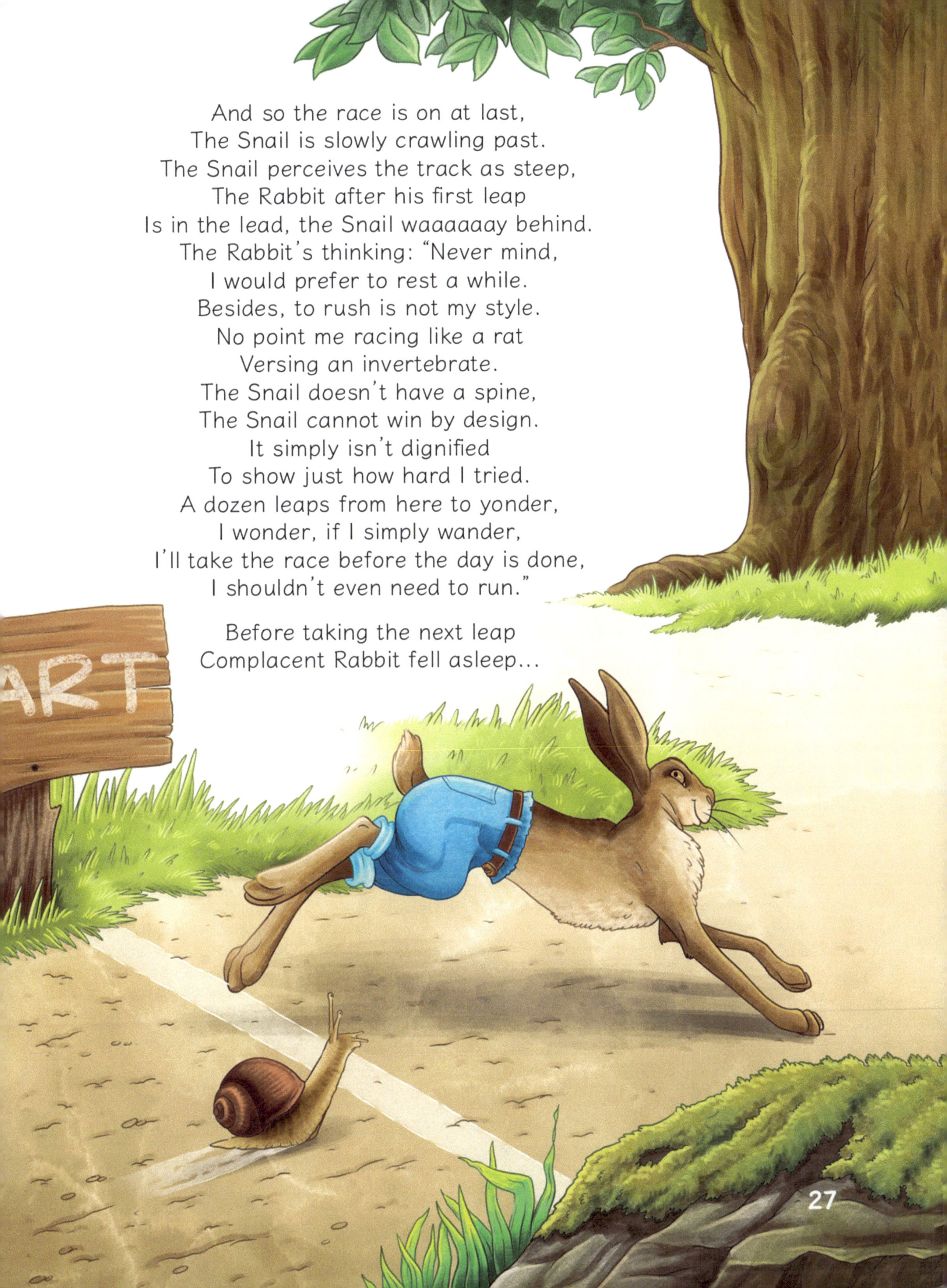

And so the race is on at last,
The Snail is slowly crawling past.
The Snail perceives the track as steep,
The Rabbit after his first leap
Is in the lead, the Snail waaaaaay behind.
The Rabbit's thinking: "Never mind,
I would prefer to rest a while.
Besides, to rush is not my style.
No point me racing like a rat
Versing an invertebrate.
The Snail doesn't have a spine,
The Snail cannot win by design.
It simply isn't dignified
To show just how hard I tried.
A dozen leaps from here to yonder,
I wonder, if I simply wander,
I'll take the race before the day is done,
I shouldn't even need to run."

Before taking the next leap
Complacent Rabbit fell asleep…

On waking up after an hour,
Recharged with energy and power,
He saw the Snail doing just fine
And just about to cross the line.

Belatedly, recharged with vengeance,
The Rabbit revved up all his engines
Stepped on the gas in leaps and bounds
To vainly make up the lost ground.

The race turned out a close-run,
The Snail crossed the line and won.
The Snail crawled the whole track
All with her house on her back.

The punters, having lost their money,
Have asked: "Who's been the real bunny?"
Some even hinted that they knew
What goes into rabbit stew.
Everyone knows disgruntled punters
Are way more dangerous than hunters.

The Rabbit, it was understood,
Would shortly leave the woods for good,
Just as promptly as he could.
They're not safe for rabbit to inhabit
Once people know about the rabbit.
Off to the Circus doing hat tricks,
Thus exercising his theatrics;
Like those endurance ads for either
Duracell or Energizer.

Being dependable, the Snail
Is now delivering the mail.
And though it may be slow
For some,
At least they know
It will come

Any race is losable
Even by the favourite,
But would you excuse a fool
If you had to pay for it?

Two Pilgrims and an Oyster

Two pilgrims out from their cloister
Walked on the beach and found an oyster.

It must be said, that very oyster
Couldn't be fresher, juicier, or moister,
Delicious, beautiful, and tempting
To eat it up until it was quite empty
To quench the appetite and thirst.

One pilgrim said: "I saw it first."
The other said: "I understand,
But I stepped on it in the sand
Before it could be even seen;
To claim it for yourself is mean."

A judge of great esteem and pride,
And reputation to decide
Such matters, happened to be by;
Was asked to judge and clarify,
In order to avoid a fight,
Determine which of them is right
And which of them is in the wrong.
To whom the oyster should belong?

The judge in order to decide
Opened the oyster, swallowed what's inside,
Said to the plaintiffs by his side:
"Your arguments are valid and
To taste the evidence at hand,
I ate the oyster and I shall
Award each one of you a shell.
That way none of the plaintiffs lost
And there will be no costs".

Your arguments may be robust and boisterous,
Instead of justice, it's easier to find more oysters.

The Swan, the Crab, and the Pike

One day, all horses went on strike.
Three friends - the Crab, the Swan, the Pike -
Then had to pull their own cart
And to immediately start.

All three work hard, they wouldn't bludge,
All three get harnessed, happy to oblige,
They pull on it but it won't budge.

The load seems light, there is no slack:
The Crab is strongly pulling back.
The Swan because he likes to fly
Is pulling up toward the sky.
The Pike because he thinks he ought to
Is pulling down to the water.

The friends are giving it
All their strength and heart.
The cart is creaking, being pulled apart.
Who's right or wrong?
Impossible to prove.
Only the cart is yet to move.

Though you be friends, between the three
Before you start it's wiser to agree.

The Ass and The Nightingale

In high esteem throughout the nation
The Nightingale's reputation
For singing was quite unsurpassed,
Until one day he met the Ass.

The Ass just being asinine,
Had trouble making up his mind.
That's why he asked the bird to sing -
Once and for all to settle things.

As for his part, the Nightingale
Being a single singing male
For whom life is but a game,
Had no qualms to sing again.

He had great stamina and will,
Thrill for reverberating trill,
Whistles, crescendos in succession,
A well composed chord progression.
With chords so passionately blessed
Plead for a mate to share his nest.

Melodious, seductive tweet
Without having missed a beat,
Combining rhythm of a lute
With mellow whistle of a flute
It was perfection absolute.
This music was enough to bless
The shepherd with his shepherdess,
The love birds were quiet and tight
Consumed by sounds of love at night.
With every animal and bird
Within cooee who could have heard,
Enchanted, magically enthralled,
It stopped the world for young and old.

Songs sung like this throughout the night
Inspire lovers till break of light
Oblivious insouciance,
Clouded, blissful nonchalance,
Out of bounds and extensions,
Defying danger and conventions,
Admiring all that heaven sent,
And wishing it would never end.

The Ass was listening
He didn't miss an ounce,
And soon was ready to pronounce:
"Well, I am not that easy to impress.
Your singing is okay, I guess.
Though, not as good as what I'm used to.
If you just listened to our Rooster...
Our Rooster is a master.
He sings much louder and faster.
The truest herald of the morn,
Lucky for us, his sounds adorn
Otherwise hard to wake up dawn.
The Rooster also has an Agent.
That Agent is himself a legend;
The Agent says our Rooster
Is now the biggest drawing new star.
The champion deserves a crown
For rousing up the whole town."

On hearing this the Nightingale
In solemn silence turned his tail
And nonchalantly flew away
To another song another day.

Any good singer would refuse to
Take singing lessons from a rooster.
Woe betide those whose class
Needs affirmation from an Ass.
No point in bearing a grudge,
Don't get an Ass to be your judge!

The Quartet

One day the Monkey on a mission
To demonstrate her skill as a musician,
Decided to set up a four-piece band
And make it the most famous in the land.

The Monkey's friends after discussion,
The Goat on strings, the Rabbit on percussion,
The Monkey in the lead, the Ass on clarinet
Agreed to call it the Quartet.

Decided: sitting should be straight,
Facing each other to coordinate
Conveniently around a stump.
They struck a tune but only heard a thump,
Snap, crackle, plop, and slump,
Followed by a loud flush.
Enough to make everyone blush.

The Monkey being the band leader,
Made a suggestion that they need a
Position that would make them sound fine,
Arrange themselves in a straight line.

Exactly how is the question.
They asked the Nightingale for a suggestion,
They said: "We have the instruments and notes,
Singing quite loud at full throat,
The Monkey's bleating like a goat.
Fortunately, we have the Ass
Who is in charge of wood and brass.
The Rabbit's on the snare drum.
The Goat's fast enough to strum.
Though plucking can't be done with hooves.
With every beat we make it proves
The team is fitting,

Most beats and notes we're hitting,
If we could only organize the sitting."

The Nightingale polite and gallant
Said to the team: "You need some talent,
Some aptitude, and heaps of training,
And then a lot of luck for entertaining.

In this line up not one of you will fit,
How you're sitting will not help a bit.
You shouldn't play, no matter how you sit."

39

The Cuckoo and the Rooster

After a dinner with sambuca,
The Rooster's cheering the Cuckoo:
"My dear Cuckoo, what a pretty voice.

It makes me tremble and rejoice
Surrounded by wondrous sounds
Graciously spreading joy around.
I'm so happy when you busk,
All day long from dawn to dusk.
Everyone knows our Cuckoo
Is a great singer and a looker."

The Cuckoo took the compliments in stride
And quite emphatically replied:
"You Rooster, are the real star,
They hear your singing near and far,
There's no one with a louder tone,
You never need a microphone.
For singing you should get the prize,
You're better than the bird of paradise!"

Chimes in the Sparrow passing by:
"Your compliments are all a lie.
We'd stop your singing if we could,
None of your singing's any good!"

What is the real explanation
For mutual but puzzling admiration?

Why, with the vigour of a seasoned spruiker,
Did our Rooster always praise the Cuckoo?

Because as a confidence and image booster
The Cuckoo's always praised the Rooster.

The Frog who wanted to be as big as the Ox

Quite unambitiously, the Frog,
Born, raised, and reared in a bog,
With his position was content
Until one formative event.
The Ox came down off the road
And overshadowed the abode
The Frog resided in thus far.
Enough to permanently scar
The Frog's fragile self-esteem,

As if the Frog's run out of steam.
The Ox was bigger than the bog,
Which deeply traumatised the Frog.
The Frog, emotionally scarred,

And in his very own backyard,
Decided to protect his turf
So inconsiderately dwarfed.

The Frog resolved he wouldn't bluff;
The Frog knew how to huff and puff.
Determined, confident, and honest,
He started puffing up in earnest.
He puffed and puffed, was getting bigger,
Admired his newly acquired figure.
New size, more substance, and street presence,
Crowd adulation, fame, and presents.
So much encouragement to puff…
His skin just wasn't thick enough.

Just one more puff caused an explosion
Resulting in much soil erosion,
Contamination of the site,
And not much left for the last rites.

Although his ego's now inflated,
The Frog's dead, buried, and cremated.

Friends, Citizens, Beware!
When there is so much hot air.

43

The Lumberjack and Death

The Lumberjack, advanced in age,
Continued working for his wage;
Deprived of fortune, wealth, or fame,
Without savings to his name
Was resolute he would cut wood
So long as possibly he could.
Bemoaning his youth long spent
Under a heavy weight was bent,

Burdened with firewood on his back
With heavy steps and heavy piled stack,
Along a winding rugged track
Towards his rundown, smoke-filled shack
Despite the odds he walked to try
To keep his home warm and dry.

The weight and pain too much to bear,
He puts the bundle down then and there.
He thinks: "Not much of life is left to spare,
Of pleasures: Nothing to declare."
His wife, his children, tax and state,
His debtors asking him to wait,
With creditors been always late,
Nothing but trouble on his plate;
Such a grim picture of his sorry state.

He's out of strength and out of breath.
Who can he call now except for Death?
And so he does in desperation,
More out of jest than expectation.

And Death doth come and stands beside
And asks him: "Did you book this ride?
Is this the ride you want to take?
I am only asking for your sake."

The Man is startled, out of his depth,
Is staring point blank at his Death.
The real thing all dressed in black
With a one-way ticket for the Lumberjack.

He says to Death: "My life's a trundle,
if you just help me with this bundle?!
I'm so sorry about this call,
I'll cancel this ride after all.
It's true,
my life couldn't get much tougher.
By now I know how to suffer.
I'm used to suffering and strife
It gives some meaning to my life."

The Goose laying golden eggs

There was a man by fortune blessed
Because a Goose that he possessed
Without prompt, without delay
Would lay a golden egg a day.
Day in day out, without fail,

They could be offered for sale
Or kept in stock for times of need.
Enough to quench anyone's greed.

The Man by storing all that gold
Amassed a quantity untold.
And yet a nagging question begs:
"What is the source of those eggs?"

With curiosity so bad,
For which the answer must be had
The Man, headstrong and now rich
To satisfy his mental itch
Cut the goose open, looked inside
For what this goose had tried to hide.
Found no trace of gold or eggs,
Just flesh and giblets, gore and dregs.

The Goose just couldn't have survived
Dissection – and was unalived.
No longer could she move or play
And clearly no more eggs to lay!

Somewhat surprisingly, of course,
The goose whilst living was the source!

Some people simply cannot rest
And put their fortune to the test.
So when you are by fortune blessed,
Then you already have what's best!!!

The Cricket and the Ant

Happy Cricket hopped along,
Singing songs all summer long.
Work just wasn't on his mind,
When he wanted he could find
Every time at every turn
Food to eat and wood to burn.

But the summer didn't last;
Hungry winter came too fast.
No more food, no place to hide,
Quickly swallowing his pride
Our Cricket asked a favour
Of the Ant, his next door neighbour:

"Please, Ant, help me if you could
To improve my singing mood
I need shelter and some food.
Let me have some grains on loan,
Just until I get my own."

"No food? Well that's a bummer.
Say, what did you do all summer?
Did you work or did you sleep?
Did you sow, did you reap?
Did you gather any grain?
Be so kind as to explain."

"I've been trying to be good
Doing things a Cricket should:
Hop and skip and fool around
In the air and on the ground,

In the grass, under a tree
Where a cricket can be free,
Doing just the things that please him.
Summer is a jolly season!
Work can ruin inspiration -
Work is not my occupation.
I just sing."

"Then take your chance.
Now you can go and dance."

About the Author

Alex Wolf Neuk is a storyteller with a mission — to reimagine Aesop's fables with the wit, satire, and poetic brilliance that Jean de La Fontaine brought to them centuries ago. A graduate of the University of New South Wales in Medicine, he is a doctor who lives in Sydney, Australia. His journey into writing took an unexpected turn when a planned trip to Paris led him to study French. What began as a practical pursuit soon became a literary challenge: to craft English versions of Aesop's fables that rival the charm and sophistication of their celebrated French adaptations.

Inspired by Rudyard Kipling's rhythmic clarity, La Fontaine's masterful irony, and Vladimir Vysotsky's acrobatic rhyming techniques, Alex Wolf Neuk breathes new life into these ancient tales. His words are vividly brought to life by the exceptional talents of illustrators Mariana Hnatenko and Alina Shabelnyk of "Nimble Pencils" team, who continue their work amidst the turmoil in Ukraine, proving that art and storytelling transcend even the harshest realities.

Beyond his literary pursuits, Alex Wolf Neuk is a devoted husband and a proud father to six wonderful children. For French readers, his work is both an homage and a challenge. For everyone else, it is an invitation to rediscover the timeless magic of fables — where wisdom, humor, and poetry meet.

With my co-authors

www.ingramcontent.com/pod-product-compliance
Lightning Source LLC
Chambersburg PA
CBHW041411300726
48978CB00002B/60